THIS BLOOMSBURY BOOK

BELONGS TO

....

To Kate, for caring so much

Bloomsbury Publishing, London, Berlin and New York

First published in Great Britain in 2009 by Bloomsbury Publishing Plc
36 Soho Square, London, W1D 3QY

Text and illustrations copyright © 2009 Michael Terry
The moral right of the author/illustrator has been asserted.

A CIP catalogue record of this book is available from the British Library

ISBN 978 0 7475 9782 7

Printed and bound in China

1 3 5 7 9 10 8 6 4 2

All papers used by Bloomsbury Publishing are natural, recyclable products
made from wood grown in well-managed forests. The manufacturing processes
conform to the environmental regulations of the country of origin.

www.bloomsbury.com

Captain Wag
and the
Polar Bears

Michael Terry

BLOOMSBURY

LONDON BERLIN NEW YORK

Captain Wag and his crew, One-Eye Jack and Old Scratch, were working on their new ship, the *Saucy Paw*, when Old Scratch saw something floating in the water.

'Look, cap'n, there be a bottle and it looks like
it's got a note inside,' shouted Old Scratch.
    'Fish it out, shipmate, and let's see what it says,'
ordered Captain Wag.

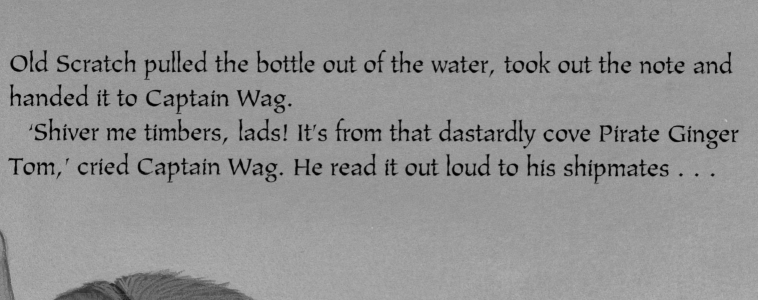

Old Scratch pulled the bottle out of the water, took out the note and handed it to Captain Wag.

'Shiver me timbers, lads! It's from that dastardly cove Pirate Ginger Tom,' cried Captain Wag. He read it out loud to his shipmates . . .

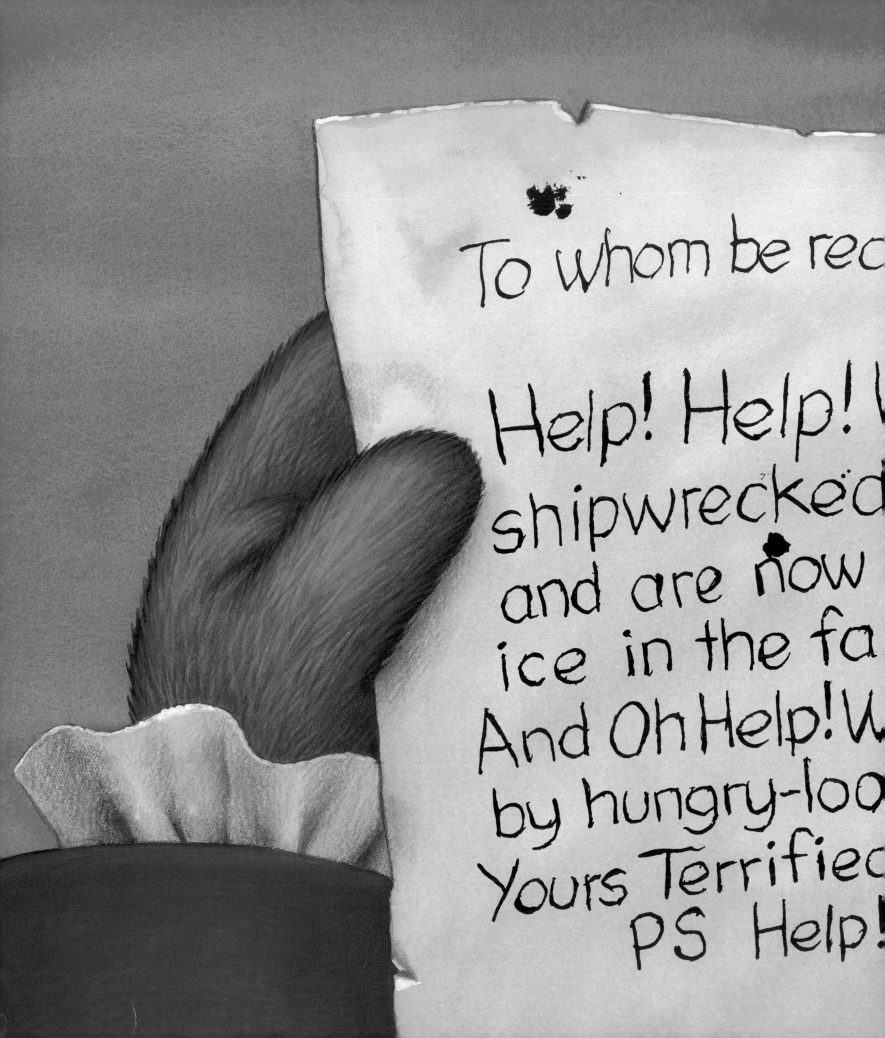

...ng this letter.

...have been
...y a whale
...randed on
...North.

...re surrounded
...ng polar bears.
...irate Ginger Tom

'Stow everything we need on board and make sure there's plenty of food and warm clothes,' said Captain Wag. 'That varmint Pirate Ginger Tom and his motley crew are in trouble and we are the only ones who can rescue them!'

As they sailed north, the weather got colder and colder. Then it started to snow so hard it became a blizzard!

The snow started to settle and cover the ship.
But as Captain Wag and his crew desperately
scraped at the snow, throwing it overboard,
the blizzard died away and the sky cleared.

Now they could see that they were surrounded by a sea of ice. Not a sound was to be heard in the freezing air. But straight ahead was a boat-shaped channel in the ice.

'That must be where Pirate Ginger Tom went!' declared Captain Wag.

They sailed between great sheets of ice, just avoiding being crushed by towering icebergs. Sometimes they would see a walrus or a seal sitting on the ice or swimming by their side.

Then they saw Pirate Ginger Tom's ship in the distance.
    As they got nearer, they could see a crowd of polar bears trying to climb on board.
    'Come on, lads! It looks like we're just in time,' cried Captain Wag.

Ginger Tom's crew were running around the deck
and up and down the rigging in fright as the
polar bears crowded around the ship, growling.
Then Ginger Tom spotted the *Saucy Paw*.
'It's a ship, lads! We're saved!'
Captain Wag and his crew came alongside.

'GET AWAY FROM THAT SHIP, YOU VARMINTS!' shouted Captain Wag to the polar bears.

The polar bears stopped what they were doing and moved towards the *Saucy Paw*. Captain Wag, One-Eye Jack and Old Scratch shook with fear as the polar bears came closer and closer.

One enormous polar bear growled, 'Who are you calling varmints?'

Captain Wag spoke up bravely. 'I am Captain Wag and we are here to save Pirate Ginger Tom and his crew from being eaten by you polar bears.'

'EATEN!' roared the bear. 'EATEN! We don't want to eat those daft cats. We just want to get this wreck off the ice. It's making such a mess — bits of wood here, bits of rope there, you can't move without tripping over something. And all those cats do is mew at us!'

Captain Wag was relieved and called up to Ginger Tom. 'AHOY THERE, GINGER TOM, YOU OLD FOOL! These bears are trying to help you, not eat you,' he said laughing. 'If you come down and lend a hand, we should be able to get your ship off this ice.'

So Ginger Tom and his crew sheepishly climbed down and, together with the polar bears, Captain Wag, One-Eye Jack and Old Scratch, they managed to push the ship off the ice.

Ginger Tom turned to Captain Wag. 'Thanks for coming to our rescue, Wag. I will not forget such a brave deed.'

'You're a rogue, Ginger Tom, but I couldn't leave you out here to freeze,' said Captain Wag, putting his arm around Ginger Tom's shoulder.

And Captain Wag and Pirate Ginger Tom laughed heartily and long together.

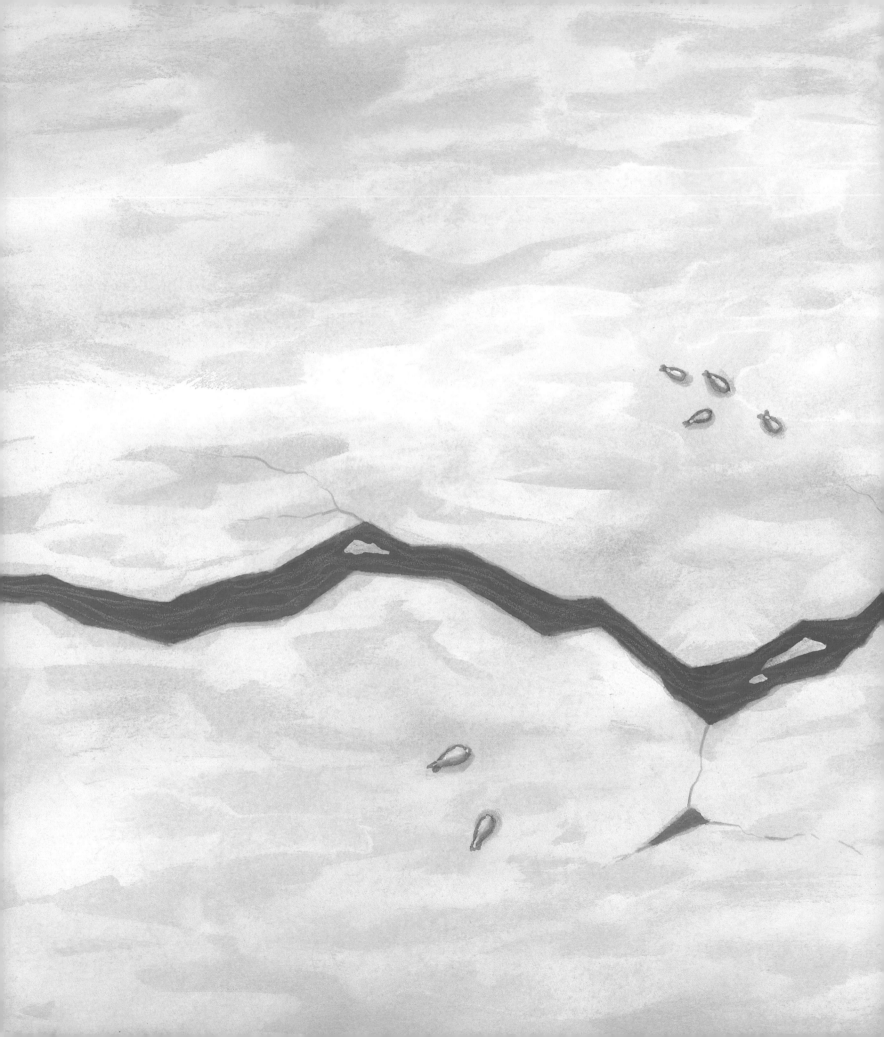

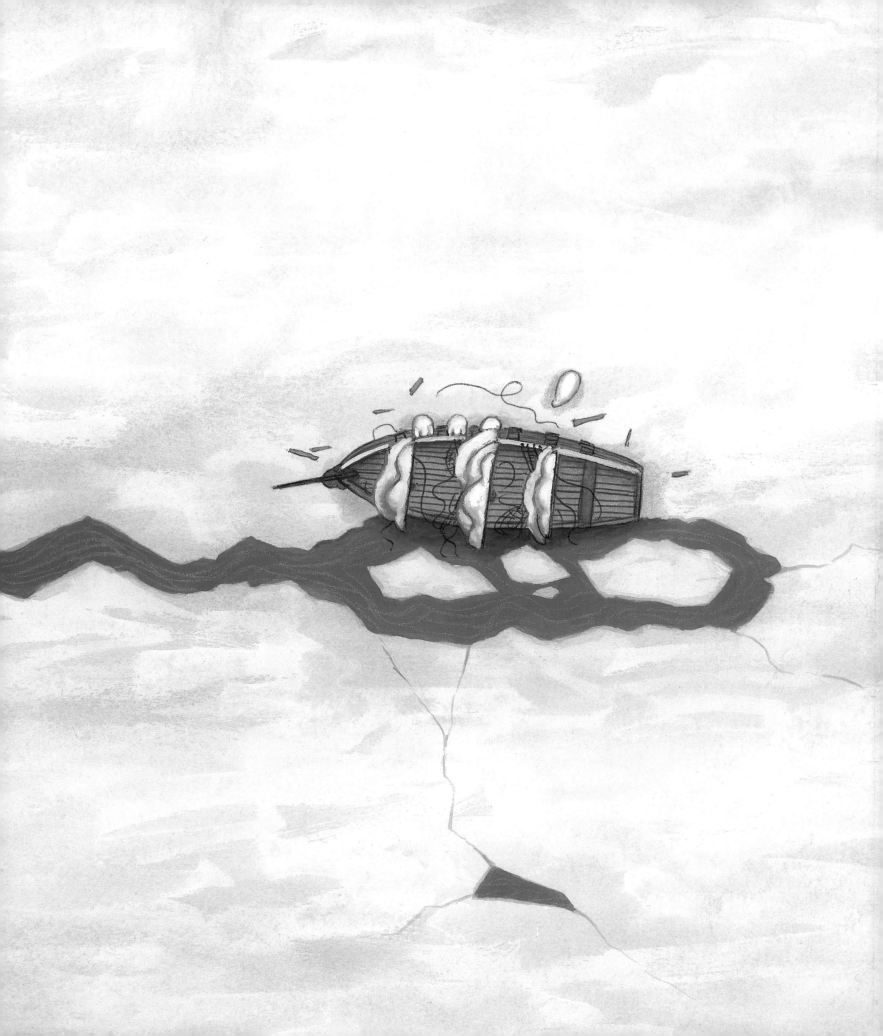